WHOBERT Whover,

Owl Detective

To Grandma Joan, who, who always knew I would be a writer
—J. G.

For Julien "Harfang," best owl detective ever
—J. P.

MARGARET K. McELDERRY BOOKS
An imprint of Simon & Schuster Children's Publishing Division
1230 Avenue of the Americas, New York, New York 10020
Text copyright © 2017 by Jason Gallaher
Illustrations copyright © 2017 by Jess Pauwels
MARGARET K. McELDERRY BOOKS is a trademark of Simon & Schuster, Inc.
For information about special discounts for bulk purchases, please contact
Simon & Schuster Special Sales at 1-866-506-1949 or business@simonandschuster.com.
The Simon & Schuster Speakers Bureau can bring authors to your live event.
For more information or to book an event, contact the Simon & Schuster Speakers Bureau at 1-866-248-3049
or visit our website at www.simonspeakers.com.
Book design by Sonia Chaghatzbanian
The text for this book was set in Minion Pro and handlettering.
The illustrations for this book were rendered in pencils, felt tip pens and digital tools.
Manufactured in China
0517 SCP   First Edition
2 4 6 8 10 9 7 5 3 1
CIP data for this book is available from the Library of Congress.
ISBN 978-1-4814-6271-6 (hardcover)
ISBN 978-1-4814-6272-3 (eBook)

JASON GALLAHER   Illustrated by JESS PAUWELS

WHOBERT Whover,

Owl Detective

MARGARET K. McELDERRY BOOKS   New York   London   Toronto   Sydney   New Delhi

WHOBERT WHOVER, Owl Detective, was on the lookout for his next case. He *always* tried to keep his neck of the woods safe.

That's when he found Perry the possum . . .
lying *awfully* still.

Whobert poked.

Whobert pushed.

Whobert pulled.

Nothing.

Whobert had found his next case.

"Poor Perry!" Whobert said.

"I will find out **who**, who done it!"

Whobert ruffled his feathers.

"I need to find a clue. A good detective
always finds a clue."

"AHA! Feathers," Whobert said. "That must mean . . .

"It was YOU!

You whacked Perry with your wicked wings!"

Debbie gasped. "What a quack! It wasn't me, Whobert! It's true!

Not guilty: you see, it was—"

"**Who?**" Whobert cried.

"**Who, who done it?** I need to find an eyewitness.

A good detective *always* finds an eyewitness.

"You there!

"Did you see what happened to poor Perry?"

"Glurgle blurp."

"This is leading nowhere."

"AHA! Perry is wet!" Whobert said. "That must mean . . . It was YOU! You soaked Perry in your sickening slime!"

Freddie croaked. "I'm *moist*, not slimy! It wasn't me, Whobert! It's true!

Not guilty: you see, it was—"

"who?" Whobert cried.

"who, who done it?"

"AHA! The getaway trail," Whobert said. "A good detective *always* follows the getaway trail."

"AHA! The trail led to the hideout!" Whobert said. "That must mean . . .

It was YOU! You thumped Perry with your terrible tail!"

Becky huffed. "Unbe*beaver*able! It wasn't me, Whobert! It's true!

Not guilty: you see, it was—"

"Who?" Whobert cried.

"Who,

WHO

could have done this to Perry?"

That's when Perry shuddered,
and shivered,
and stood straight up!
"It was *you!*" Perry shouted.

"Perry! You're alive!" Whobert said. "But what's all this nonsense about *me* being the culprit? It wasn't me, Perry! It's true! Not guilty: you see, it was—"

"YOU!"

Perry said. "You scared me! Your terrifying talons gave me such a fright, I played dead. That's what possums *do*."

Whobert laughed. "Terrifying talons? These are just my feet.
They're used for perching atop trees as I look for evildoers. See?"
Whobert proudly flashed his talons.

Unfortunately, Perry wasn't expecting this.

"Poor Perry!" Whobert said. "I will find out **who**, who done it!"